# ZPL

BY
SCOTT SONNEBORN

ILLUSTRATED BY
OMAR LOZANO

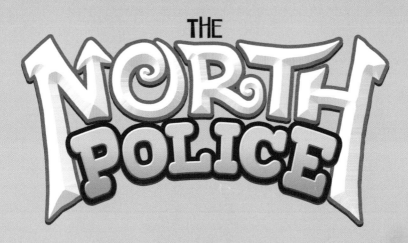

THE NORTH POLICE

# Reindeer Games

PICTURE WINDOW BOOKS
A CAPSTONE IMPRINT

The North Police is published by
Picture Window Books
a Capstone Imprint
1710 Roe Crest Drive
North Mankato, Minnesota 56003
www.capstonepub.com

Cataloging-in-Publication Data is available at the Library of Congress website.
ISBN: 978-1-4795-6487-3 (library binding)
ISBN: 978-1-4747-0034-4 (paperback)
ISBN: 978-1-4795-8478-9 (eBook)

Summary: The North Police are on the case at the annual Reindeer Games. When
a reindeer is injured, they must find out who's to blame. The North Pole's greatest
detectives will need a Christmas miracle to solve this reindeer riddle!

Designer: Bob Lentz

Printed in China by Nordica
0415/CA21500537
042015   008843NORDF15

# TABLE OF CONTENTS

**(NORTH POHL-eess)**

The North Police are

the elves who solve crimes

at the North Pole.

**These are their stories . . .**

## CHAPTER 1
# Red-nosed
# Reindeer

It was a bright, cold

morning in Christmas Town.

In the North Police station,

the chief shouted, "Detectives

Sprinkles and Sugarplum!

Get in my office! Now!"

Sitting beside the chief was
an unhappy reindeer. He had
a shiny red nose.

"What happened to your
nose?" asked Sugarplum.

"I was playing in the
Reindeer Games," said the
reindeer. "Then — WHAM! —
someone bopped me with a
snowboard. I lost the race and
got this red mark."

"Now they won't let this red-nosed reindeer join in any Reindeer Games," the chief told Sprinkles and Sugarplum. "Competing hurt is against the rules."

"Whoever wins the Games joins Donner, Blitzen, and the others pulling Santa's sleigh," said the reindeer. "I was in first place."

"Do you think another
reindeer knocked you out
of the Games on purpose?"
asked Detective Sugarplum.
"This case sounds stickier
than a wet candy cane!"

"That's why I'm putting my two best detectives on the case," the chief replied. "I'm sending you both to the Reindeer Games . . . undercover!"

## CHAPTER 2
# Reindeer Games

At the Games, two

reindeer raced on skates.

Another pair wrestled with

their antlers.

One reindeer swayed on

wobbly legs.

"Hey, look at him!" said

a mean-looking reindeer,

pointing at the wobbly one.

All the other reindeer

laughed and called him

names.

They didn't know it, but there was a good reason the wobbly reindeer couldn't stand straight. It was the North Police in disguise!

"I don't know if this plan will work," said Sprinkles. "We can't even stand, much less play Reindeer Games!"

"That's why it's going to work." Sugarplum smiled.

The mean reindeer slid over on her snowboard. "Let's race," she said. "You look like you'll be easy to beat!"

The North Police tried to climb onto a snowboard.

"Whoa!" cried Sugarplum and Sprinkles. They slipped and fell into the snow.

"This isn't fair," Detective Sprinkles told the mean reindeer. "You'll win easily."

"I don't care about fair!" said the mean reindeer. "I just want to win!"

Lying on the ground, the North Police saw the bottom of the reindeer's snowboard.

It was bright red — except for a nose-shaped mark of missing paint.

"We caught you red-handed!" said Sugarplum.

"Well, red-BOARDED,"

corrected Sprinkles.

"Huh?" asked the mean

reindeer, confused.

ZIPPP! The elves removed

their disguise.

"The North Police!" the

mean reindeer shouted.

And with that, she flew

into the air!

## Chapter 3
# The Saint Nick of Time

"Roasted chestnuts!"

shouted Sprinkles, watching

the reindeer zoom away.

Sugarplum flashed her

badge. Then she hitched a

ride on a nearby reindeer.

The North Police detectives

WHOOOOSHED through the

sky. Soon, they spotted the

suspect.

"I'm getting too old for

this!" cried Sprinkles.

"Don't be silly," replied
Sugarplum. "You're only
three hundred and twelve."

She grabbed Sprinkles's
arm and jumped!

The North Police landed right atop the mean reindeer. Sugarplum slapped her cuffs on the reindeer's legs.

"We did it!" cried Detective Sprinkles.

"You did it, all right!" said the mean reindeer. "I can't fly with handcuffs on!"

"Ahhh!" they all shouted, tumbling out of the sky.

"Ho, ho, hold on!" cried a voice. It was Santa!

He caught the North Police and the reindeer in his sleigh. "Looks like I got here in the Saint Nick of time!" he said.

"Thanks, Santa," said Detective Sprinkles.

"Thank you," said Santa. "Without you, I would've had a cheater pulling my sleigh this Christmas."

"Just doing our jobs," said Sugarplum.

"Hooray for the North Police!" said Santa.

"Hooray!" everyone shouted out with glee.

# CASE CLOSED!

6' 6"
6' 0"
5' 6"
5' 0"
4' 6"
4' 0"
3' 6"

CASE 004    NORTH POLICE
## SPIKE
Reindeer • Height 5'8" • Weight 175

# GLOSSARY

**badge** (BAJ) — a small metal shield worn by officers so other people know they are police

**cuffs** (KUHFS) — metal rings joined by a chain that are locked on a criminal's wrists to stop them from escaping

**detective** (di-TEK-tiv) — one who investigates crimes

**disguise** (diss-GIZE) — a costume worn to hide what someone really looks like

**suspect** (SUH-spekt) — someone thought to be involved in a crime

# These are their stories . . .

**only from**
PICTURE WINDOW BOOKS!

## AUTHOR

Scott Sonneborn has written dozens of books, one circus (for Ringling Bros. Barnum & Bailey), and a bunch of TV shows. He's been nominated for one Emmy and spent three very cool years working at DC Comics. He lives in Los Angeles with his wife and their two sons.

## ILLUSTRATOR

Omar Lozano lives in Monterrey, Mexico. He has always been crazy for illustration, constantly on the lookout for awesome things to draw. In his free time, he watches lots of movies, reads fantasy and sci-fi books, and draws! Omar has worked for Marvel, DC, IDW, Capstone, and more.

11/15